Max the Mucky Puppy

"Max!" Simon yelled. "Keep away from those cowpats!"

Too late . . .

Max had already dived into the nearest cowpat and was rolling around, enjoying himself enormously.

Simon dashed over to Max. Holding his nose, he grabbed the puppy's collar and pulled him out.

"Max, you *stink*!" Simon groaned. "We're in for it now!"

Titles in Jenny Dale's PUPPY TALES™ series

All of Jenny Dale's PUPPY TALES books can
be ordered at your local bookshop or are
available by post from Bookpost
(tel: 01624 677237)

Max the Mucky Puppy

by Jenny Dale

Illustrated by Frank Rodgers

A Working Partners Book

MACMILLAN CHILDREN'S BOOKS

Special thanks to Narinder Dhami

First published 1999 by Macmillan Children's Books
a division of Macmillan Publishers Limited
20 New Wharf Road, London N1 9RR
Basingstoke and Oxford
www.panmacmillan.com

Associated companies throughout the world

Created by Working Partners Limited
London W12 7QY

ISBN 0 330 37363 3

11 13 15 17 19 18 16 14 12

A CIP catalogue record for this book is available from
the British Library.

Printed and bound in Great Britain by Mackays of Chatham plc, Kent

Chapter One

"Max, you're filthy!" Simon yelled. "And you smell *horrible*!"

Max, who was sniffing around in a hedgerow, looked up at Simon, his brown eyes puzzled. He'd only rolled around in a muddy puddle. What was wrong with that? Max thought he smelled *great*!

Simon took Max's lead out of his coat pocket and grabbed his wet and muddy puppy. "Max, you've got to be the muckiest pup in the whole world!" he said, shaking his head. "Come on, let's go home."

Max jumped up eagerly at Simon's legs, wagging his short, stumpy tail furiously. Simon looked down at the muddy paw-prints Max had left all over his jeans. "Ma-ax!" he moaned as he clipped the puppy's lead to his collar. "You'll have to go straight in the bath again when we get back!"

Max's tail stopped wagging. Bath! He'd come to hate hearing that word. All the nice smells

he'd collected during their walk
would be washed away. Simon
and his mum always used a
shampoo on him too, which
smelled nasty and made Max
sneeze. Max hung his head and
whined all the way home.

Mrs Green, Simon's mum, was
in the back garden. "Not *again*!"
she cried when she saw Max.

"He'll have to go straight into the bath! I'll go and get it ready."

"I don't want a bath!" Max barked crossly. But Mrs Green took no notice and marched off into the house. Max decided that as soon as Simon let him off the lead, he'd shoot upstairs and hide under one of the beds. They'd never find him there!

"And don't let him off the lead, Simon!" Mrs Green called as she hurried up to the bathroom. "He'll only hide under one of the beds, and then we'll never get him out!"

"Huh! Foiled again!" Max snuffled and whined then slumped to the floor, feeling very miserable. It was always the same. Max just couldn't understand it. He was always careful to roll in only the best muck, mud and puddles he could find. But the Greens were never satisfied. They were always wanting to wash him!

"Never mind, Max," said Simon, kneeling down to stroke Max's head. "You had to have a bath anyway. We're taking you to the dog show tomorrow."

Max licked Simon's hand gloomily. He didn't know what a dog show was, but if he had to have a bath to go there, he was pretty sure he wasn't going to like it.

"Simon, you can bring Max up now," called Mrs Green.

Max refused to budge so Simon

had to carry him. Mrs Green was waiting for them in the bathroom with her sleeves rolled up.

"In you go, Max!" she said, lowering the puppy's sturdy little body into the bathtub. "We'll soon have you nice and clean again!"

Max knew when he was beaten. He sat sulking while Simon splashed warm water over his coat. Then Mrs Green reached for a big bottle and unscrewed the lid.

Max's heart sank. "Oh no, not the shampoo!" he woofed crossly. But Mrs Green took no notice.

"You're going to smell lovely and clean afterwards, Max," Simon told him as his mum poured a dollop of shampoo into her hand then began to rub it briskly into Max's coat.

"Pooh! That smells *horrible*!" Max yelped, sneezing loudly.

"Be quiet, Max!" said Mrs Green sternly as she and Simon shampooed his shaggy coat.

"You want to look nice for the

dog show tomorrow, don't you, Max?" said Simon.

"I looked nice *before*!" Max woofed back grumpily. Then he yelped again as the shower spray was turned on him and water went up his nose.

"I think you might win a prize tomorrow, Max," said Simon as he lifted his puppy out of the bath and began to dry him with an old towel.

Max didn't know what a prize was, and he didn't care. He was fed up! He'd have to smell of that pongy shampoo until Simon took him out for a walk again tomorrow morning. Max thought of all the mucky places he could visit along his favourite muddy lane.

He could hardly wait.

"You'll have to keep Max clean tomorrow, Simon," Mrs Green said. "He mustn't get dirty again before the dog show, so don't let him off the lead."

Max's ears pricked up. This was terrible! Was he going to have to smell like this *all day* tomorrow? Just to go to some silly dog show – whatever *that* was? It wasn't fair!

Chapter Two

"No, Max!" Simon said firmly the following morning. "I *can't* let you off the lead – you heard what Mum said!"

Max looked up at Simon, pleading with his big brown eyes. He whined and pawed at Simon's leg.

"Well . . ." Simon looked down at his puppy. "Just for a little while, then. But you've got to stay close to me."

Max sat quietly while Simon unclipped his lead. Then he shot off like a rocket. He just couldn't stop himself!

"Max! Max! Come back!" Simon shouted.

Max took no notice as he galloped happily down the lane, through three huge, dirty puddles – *splash, splash, splash!* – one after the other. The last one was so deep that the water came up to Max's tummy. Max gave himself a delighted shake, then had a quick roll in the dirty water.

"Max, come here!" Simon cried,

as he ran after the excited puppy.
"Mum's going to be *really* mad,
now!"

Max raced off again, sniffing as
he went. Over in a nearby field
there was a wonderful smell –
one of his favourites. *Cows.*

Max was scared of cows because
they were so big, but cowpats
were fun!

He stuck his head through a gate and looked into the field. To his delight, the cows were being led away by the farmer to be milked. He wriggled under the gate and whisked out of reach, just as Simon made a grab for him.

"Max!" Simon yelled, as he watched his puppy run across the field. "Keep away from those cowpats!"

Too late . . .

Max had already dived into the nearest cowpat and was rolling around, enjoying himself enormously.

Simon climbed over the gate and dashed up to Max. Holding his nose, Simon grabbed the puppy's collar and pulled him out.

"Max, you *stink*!" Simon groaned. "We're in for it now!"

"Simon! I thought I told you to keep him clean!" Mrs Green gasped, when Simon and Max arrived home.

"Sorry, Mum," Simon muttered.

Mrs Green bent down to Max to tell him off. "Max, you're a very naughty—" She stopped and sniffed, then stepped away. "Is that . . .?"

Simon nodded unhappily. "Yes, he rolled in a cowpat!"

Max sat down on the path, feeling pleased with himself. He thought he smelled fantastic!

"He can't come into the house like that!" Mrs Green snapped. "And we've got to go shopping now. He'll have to stay out in the back garden."

"But what about the dog show?" Simon asked anxiously.

His mum glanced at her watch. "If we give Max another bath as soon as we get back from shopping, we should get to the show just in time," she said.

Max woofed in disgust. *Another* bath?

Simon shut Max in the back garden, then he and his mum went out shopping.

Max looked around the garden, feeling very sorry for himself. He brightened up when he noticed a

couple of muddy puddles.
"Might as well make the most
of them before my bath," he
woofed.

Max rolled about in puddles for
a while, and then snuffled around
in the compost heap in the corner
of the garden. Then suddenly he
smelt something horrible. A
soapy, sneezy smell. Shampoo!
He wondered where it was
coming from and rushed over to
the fence to find out. One of the
wooden boards was broken at the
bottom and Max could push his
head through to see down the
lane.

Missy, the white poodle who
lived a few doors away, was
trotting towards him with her

owner, Mrs Naylor. Missy's fluffy coat was gleaming white and she was wearing a red bow on top of her head.

Max had never seen a dog wearing a bow before. "Why are you wearing that thing on your head?" he barked. "You look really silly!"

"It makes me look pretty," Missy yapped haughtily. She looked down her nose at Max. "Not like you!"

Max sniffed and sneezed. "You've had a bath, too," he woofed. "Poor you!" He knew that Missy liked to get mucky too. But she didn't often get the chance – Missy's owner was much stricter than Simon.

"Well, I'm going to the dog show, so I have to look nice." Missy stuck her little black nose in the air. "It's usually worth it in the end!" she added rather mysteriously.

"Oh, I'm going to the dog show too!" Max barked. But he hoped that Simon wouldn't want *him* to wear a silly ribbon on his head! "What *is* a dog show anyway?"

"Don't you know *anything*?" Missy yapped. "All the dogs walk up and down and then the judges choose the best one," she explained.

"Oh." Max preened himself. He *must* be in with a good chance!

Missy looked down her nose again. "But to be a winner you

have to be clean and smell nice
to people. And you don't!" she
barked.

Max sniffed. "But I smell
lovely!" he barked back.

"Not to people, you don't,"
Missy replied.

Mrs Naylor was becoming
impatient and dragged Missy on
down the lane.

"You won't win," Missy barked over her shoulder. "Not like that!"

"We'll see!" Max growled crossly. He had made a decision. He wouldn't wait for Simon and Mrs Green to come home and give him another nasty bath. No, he'd go to the dog show right now!

Chapter Three

Max had never tried to squeeze
through the hole in the fence
before. It looked too small. But he
was determined to go and check
out the dog show.

   Max's head went through the
hole easily enough. So did his
two front legs. But then his

26

tummy got stuck. He yelped in panic and wriggled hard. Luckily the wood around the hole was rotting away and it broke. Max tumbled out onto the pavement. Phew! He picked himself up and looked down the lane.

Missy and Mrs Naylor were just disappearing round the corner, so Max galloped after them. Keeping out of sight, he followed them until they came to the park. Max often went to the park with Simon at weekends, but today everything looked completely different.

There were huge white tents set up on the grass, and lots of stalls, selling all kinds of doggy things like leads and toys and baskets and dog food. The sun had come out at last. Crowds of people walked around with their dogs, having fun and eating ice creams. Max wagged his tail. This all looked very exciting!

Missy and Mrs Naylor were making their way over to the biggest tent. Max followed them. A short man and a tall woman were sitting at a table near the entrance. Mrs Naylor stopped to speak with them, then she and Missy went inside.

Max loped after them, but the man at the table reached down and grabbed the puppy by his collar. "And where do you think you're going?" he asked fiercely.

Max was a bit frightened. He thought he'd better play safe so he rolled over onto his back to show the man his cute tummy. It always worked with Mrs Green.

But the fierce man didn't seem very impressed. And neither did the woman.

"He's filthy!" she said. "Absolutely filthy!"

"He's got a tag on his collar.

Maybe we should call his owners and tell them to come and collect him," said the man with a frown. Then he sniffed the air. "What *is* that awful smell?"

The woman came over and sniffed too. She made a face. "Oh, he smells horrible!"

The man let go of Max's collar very quickly.

Max didn't wait to hear any more. He escaped, racing off around the side of the tent, then snuffled around, wondering what to do. Then he began to feel angry. If those silly people wouldn't let him into the dog show, he'd have to find his own way in!

Using his nose, Max managed to lift up the edge of the canvas. He stuck his head in and looked around. There was so much going on that no one noticed him. In the middle of the tent was a big ring. Inside it, people and dogs were walking up and down, and lots of other people were sitting on benches, watching.

Max wriggled under the canvas and into the tent. The dogs in the ring were now lining up and a man was walking up and down, looking them over. Max was amazed to see that all the dogs were just as well washed and brushed as Missy.

Suddenly a delicious smell wafted by. Max sniffed hard. *Tasty Chews!* He could smell his favourite snack!

The puppy decided to go and find out where the smell of Tasty Chews was coming from. Perhaps he could grab a few. He trotted off around the tent.

"What *is* that smell?" asked a woman watching the dog show, as Max went past.

"I don't know," said the man next to her, looking around. "But it's disgusting!"

As Max walked on, more and more people began to pull faces and hold their noses. But Max was too busy sniffing his way to the Tasty Chews.

There they were! There were huge bags of Tasty Chews on a stall in the corner of the tent. As Max watched, a dog and his owner went up to the stall and the nice lady behind the counter gave the dog a Tasty Chew to try.

Max's mouth watered and dribbled onto the grass. He looked up longingly at the plate. It was much too high for him to reach. But he had to get a Tasty Chew somehow.

The stallholder turned to serve a customer. Then Max noticed an enormous bag of dog biscuits lying on its side on the ground next to the stall. Max wagged his tail. He had an idea . . .

While the stallholder wasn't looking, Max scrabbled up onto the bag of dog biscuits, put his front paws against the stall and, straining upwards, just managed to grab a Tasty Chew in his mouth. He gave it a sharp tug . . . and the whole plate of chews flew off the table and onto the grass.

"Aargh!" screamed the stall-holder. "Look what that dog's done! And what's that *awful* smell?"

Clutching his chew firmly in his mouth, Max beat a hasty retreat. He dived under one of the benches around the ring to eat his snack in peace.

"Mummy, what's that nasty smell?" asked a little girl who was sitting on the bench, watching the dog show.

"I don't know," said her mother with a frown. "Let's move to another seat!"

Max quickly finished his chew, and then decided to go and see what the dogs in the ring were doing. He wriggled out from under the bench and trotted across the tent.

But before he got very far, a hand suddenly grabbed hold of

his collar and held him tightly.

"Can someone *please* tell me who this dog belongs to?" asked a stern voice.

Chapter Four

A grim-faced lady, wearing a big, scary, flowery hat, was holding Max's collar. Her grip was too tight for him to roll over and try his cute tummy trick on her.

"Who owns this dog?" the woman said in a loud voice. "He

shouldn't be wandering around
without his lead on!"

Everyone stared at Max dis-
approvingly. He was beginning
to feel very embarrassed.

"That's the dog which knocked
over my 'free samples' plate!"
called the woman from the Tasty
Chews stall.

"I think I'd better take you to

the lost property tent," said the scary woman.

Max whined and tried to drag himself free. He didn't want to be taken *anywhere*. He wanted to stay and watch the dog show.

"I really don't know what your owner is thinking of," the woman went on, as she pulled Max away from the ring. Then she sniffed the air. "What *is* that awful smell? Is it you?"

She bent over the puppy to sniff him. As she did so, her big, flowery hat fell off her head and landed right on top of Max. The woman was so surprised that she let go of his collar. Max took off at top speed, still wearing the flowery hat.

"My hat!" the woman shrieked.
"That dog's run off with my hat!"

Max couldn't see where he was
going. The hat was so big it
almost covered him completely.
He shook himself hard. The hat
flew off his head, and Max shot
under a bench out of sight.

The puppy was panting, but he
tried to do it quietly so no one
would know he was there. He

peeped out from under the bench and saw a boy pick up the hat and give it back to the woman. The hat was now mucky and covered in bits of grass. Max saw the woman sniff it and pull a face.

Max was about to bark indignantly, then remembered he was hiding. It was an ugly hat anyway! He slumped down on the grass, wondering what to do now.

Suddenly everyone around the ring started applauding. Max wriggled forward on his tummy to see what was going on.

A line of poodles like Missy were trotting into the ring with their owners. Max's ears pricked up. Missy was there too, with her shiny red bow. Several of the other poodles also wore bows on their head. All of them were squeaky clean and their coats gleamed. But what a pong all those shampooed coats made!

Max decided to go into the ring and say hello to Missy. He took a quick look to make sure the scary hat woman wasn't around, then wriggled out of his hiding place.

The poodles in the ring were now sitting quietly beside their owners. Missy and Mrs Naylor were at the end of the line, and Max raced up to them with a friendly woof.

"Max! What are *you* doing here?" Missy barked, looking shocked.

"I wanted to see what the dog show was like," Max barked back.

"Go away!" Missy yapped crossly. "The judge is about to choose the winner!"

Just then Mrs Naylor glanced down and saw scruffy, filthy Max sitting next to Missy. She gave a little scream.

"It's me – Max!" Max barked.

"Go away!" she snapped, flapping her hands at Max. "You'll get Missy all dirty!"

"Yes, go away!" Missy barked. "Can't you see? Everyone's laughing at you!"

Max looked round the ring. All the people watching really were laughing and pointing at him. Suddenly Max felt very small and

lonely, sitting there without his owner. He wished that Simon was with him.

The judge was now walking along, inspecting the line of dogs. Max's heart began to thump fast again. It was the scary hat woman! He had to get out of there before she saw him!

Max dashed across the ring and wriggled his way under the benches. He could hear people talking about him.

"That dog needs a bath – he stinks!"

"Poor little thing! His owner doesn't look after him properly."

"People who neglect their dogs like that shouldn't be allowed to have one."

Max barked crossly as he rushed past. "Simon's a brilliant owner!" But no one took any notice.

The poor pup was very fed up. Everyone had laughed at him and now they were saying nasty things about Simon, who was the best owner in the world. Max decided gloomily that he definitely didn't like dog shows.

". . . And the first prize goes to Missy and Mrs Naylor!" boomed the scary hat woman. "Missy wins a beautiful silver cup. And from our sponsors, a year's supply of Tasty Chews!"

As the judge handed over the silver cup to Mrs Naylor and Missy, everyone began to applaud. But Max didn't care about a boring old cup. He was thinking about a whole year's supply of Tasty Chews. Maybe he should enter the dog show after all!

Chapter Five

Max ran home from the park as
fast as his legs could carry him.
He had to get back before Simon
and Mrs Green returned from
shopping, or there wouldn't be
time for him to have a bath and
enter the dog show. Max was so
determined to get his paws on

those Tasty Chews that he could hardly wait to dive into a tub of warm water and be smothered from head to tail in pongy bubbles. What were a few sneezes if he could win a mountain of Tasty Chews?

Max charged up to the Greens' back garden, and squeezed his way through the hole in the fence. Then he bounded over to the back door and looked up through the kitchen window. There was no sign of Simon and his mum. Max wagged his tail happily. That meant he'd got back in time.

A few moments later, Simon and Mrs Green arrived home. Max began to whine and scratch impatiently at the kitchen door.

"Hello, boy!" said Simon, opening it.

"Don't let him in yet . . ." Mrs Green began. But it was too late. Max had already dashed past them and was racing up the stairs at top speed.

"Oh no, he's probably gone to hide under one of the beds!" Mrs

Green groaned. "We'll never get him out now!"

Simon and Mrs Green hurried upstairs after Max. They checked under all the beds but there was no sign of him.

Max woofed. "In here!"

Simon rushed into the bathroom and found Max standing with his front paws on the rim of the bath, wagging his tail. "I think Max actually *wants* to have a bath!" Simon said, laughing.

"Quick, let's get him into the tub before he changes his mind!" said Mrs Green, sounding amazed.

Instead of wriggling about like he usually did, Max sat still while he was being washed. He didn't even move when Simon sprayed him with water. But he couldn't stop himself sneezing when a bubble popped on his nose.

After Simon had finished rinsing away the suds, he lifted Max out of the bath and rubbed him quickly with the puppy's old towel.

"Use my hairdryer to speed things up, Simon," Mrs Green suggested.

Max was trying so hard to be good, he didn't even bark at the hairdryer like he usually did when it was switched on. He sat there while the hot air flew over his coat, drying it very fast.

"What do you think, Max?" Simon asked, holding Max up to the bathroom mirror.

Max looked at his reflection and

yelped in alarm. His coat, blown
dry by the hairdryer, had never
been so fluffy! He didn't like it
one bit.

Still, looking so silly was in a
good cause, Max told himself. It
would all be worth it if he won
those Tasty Chews. He just hoped
he didn't meet any of his doggy
friends on the way!

"We must go, or we'll be too late to enter Max," said Mrs Green.

Simon put Max's lead on, and they all hurried off to the dog show.

By the time they arrived at the park, Max was feeling nervous. All the pups he had seen before were much more smart than him. He didn't remember seeing any dogs like himself at the show. Maybe Simon and Mrs Green had made a mistake. Maybe everyone in the audience would laugh at him again if he went into the ring with all those posh pups . . .

Simon and Mrs Green took Max over to the tent and stopped at the table where the fierce man and woman were still guarding the entrance.

"I'm Simon Green, and this is Max," said Simon. "We're entering the Cutest Puppy Competition."

Max's ears pricked up. Cutest Puppy? Well, he might not be a posh pup, but he *was* quite cute!

"Oh, what a sweetie!" said the woman, bending down to pat Max. Then she frowned. "Funny, he looks familiar . . ."

"Yes, he does," the man agreed. "I'm sure I've seen him before . . ."

Feeling alarmed, Max scuttled out of sight behind Simon's legs. If anyone recognised him as the pup who'd caused all the trouble earlier, he might not be allowed to enter the competition!

Chapter Six

"Will all entrants in the Cutest Puppy competition please make their way into the ring?"

"That's us, Mum!" Simon said as the announcement came over the loudspeaker.

"Good luck!" said Mrs Green, giving Max a pat on the head.

Max was nervous as he trotted into the ring next to Simon. He just hoped the scary hat woman didn't see him. He really wanted to win all those lovely Tasty Chews *and* show everyone what a brilliant owner Simon was.

As he and Simon walked around the ring, Max took a look at the other entrants. There were all kinds of puppies – other mongrels like Max, as well as posh pedigrees. Max trotted along with his head held high and his tail wagging hard from side to side. He was determined to be cuter than *any* of the other puppies.

After they'd walked round the ring, all the puppies and their

owners lined up, ready to be
inspected.

"Here's the judge, Max," Simon
whispered.

Max looked across the ring at
the person walking slowly down
the line of puppies, looking them
over. His heart sank. "Oh, no!" he
whimpered. It was the scary hat
woman!

"Try to be good, Max," Simon said, patting Max's head. Max gave Simon's hand a quick lick.

But the puppy was shaking a little as the judge came nearer. Would she recognise him?

"What a lovely little puppy! You clearly look after him very well," the judge said to Simon. She smiled down at Max, then made a note on her clipboard. Max allowed his tail to wag, just a little. It looked as if he was going to get away with it! "Hmm . . ." the judge went on. "He seems familiar. Could I have seen him before?" Max's tail stopped wagging.

Simon shook his head. "No," he replied. "This is the first time Max has been to a dog show."

"That's what *you* think," Max whimpered quietly.

The judge didn't say anything else. She walked back down the line of puppies, making notes and thinking hard. Then she announced with a smile, "The winner in the Cutest Puppy competition is . . . Max, who's owned by Simon Green!"

"Max! We won!" Simon yelled, swinging the puppy up into his arms as the audience clapped loudly. *"We won!"*

Max barked his head off. They'd done it! He was officially the cutest puppy! Now, where was his mountain of Tasty Chews?

The judge presented Simon and Max with a small silver cup.

"Well done," she said. "And, of course, that isn't all you get!"

Here it comes, Max thought, licking his lips.

"You also get a year's supply of Doggy Delight Shampoo!" the judge went on, and the audience clapped again.

Shampoo? Max could hardly believe his ears! *Doggy Delight*

Shampoo? Where were his Tasty Chews?

"Aren't you clever, Max?" said a delighted Mrs Green, as Simon rushed over to her with Max and the silver cup in his arms. "Now we won't have to buy any shampoo for a year!"

"Oh, great!" Max yapped sulkily.

"Mum, can we buy Max some special treats because he won?" Simon asked. Max's ears pricked up. *That* was more like it!

"Of course we can," Simon's mum agreed.

As they went over to the Tasty Chews stall, lots of people wanted to pat and stroke Max and tell him what a lovely pup he was. Simon looked very proud and, even though he hadn't won the Tasty Chews, Max began to cheer up. Maybe it wasn't so bad to be clean and smell "nice" if he got so much fuss!

"What can I get you?" asked the woman behind the stall.

"We'll have a big bag of Tasty Chews, please," said Simon. "They're Max's favourite!"

"He's a lovely pup!" said the woman with a smile. Then she frowned. "Funny, he looks familiar . . ."

"See, Max?" Simon said happily as they walked home from the dog show. "Being clean *isn't* so bad after all, is it?

But Max wasn't listening. He'd just spotted an *enormous* muddy puddle . . .